FASTER, FASTER!

For Isabelle

FASTER, FASTER!
A RED FOX BOOK 978 1 782 95571 9

First published in Great Britain by Julia MacRae,
an imprint of Random House Children's Publishers UK
A Random House Group Company

Julia MacRae edition published as *Faster, Faster, Little Red Train* 1999
Red Fox edition published as *Faster, Faster, Little Red Train* 2000
Red Fox edition re-issued 2009

19

Copyright © Benedict Blathwayt, 1999

The right of Benedict Blathwayt to be identified as the author and illustrator of this work
has been asserted in accordance with the Copyright, Designs and Patents Act 1988.

Red Fox Books are published by Random House Children's Publishers UK ,
61–63 Uxbridge Road, London W5 5SA

www.**randomhouse**.co.uk
www.**randomhousechildrens**.co.uk

Addresses for companies within The Random House Group Limited can be found at:
www.randomhouse.co.uk/offices.htm

THE RANDOM HOUSE GROUP Limited Reg. No. 954009

A CIP catalogue record for this book is available from the British Library.

Printed in China

LITTLE RED TRAIN

FASTER, FASTER!

Benedict Blathwayt

RED FOX

Duffy Driver was eating his
breakfast when the telephone rang.
"The fast train to Pebblecombe has
broken down," he said. "The Little
Red Train is needed. I'll have to rush."

The passengers from the broken-down train were cross and worried. "Will the Little Red Train get there on time, we don't want to miss the fair!"
"All aboard for Pebblecombe," called Duffy Driver.
"We'll go as fast as we can!"
Chuff chuff went the Little Red Train.
Click clack went the wheels on the track.

Their first stop was Newtown.

"Who's for Pebblecombe fair?" shouted Duffy Driver.

"Quick as you can!"

A lady with a big box of strawberries climbed on board.

Whoosh went the steam from the Little Red Train.

Click clack went the wheels on the track.

Click clack clicketty clack.

Next they stopped at Woodhaven.

"Jump on for Pebblecombe fair!" shouted Duffy Driver.

A man with a crate of hens squeezed into the carriage.

"You're running late," he grumbled.

"We're doing our best," Duffy Driver said cheerfully.

Chuff chuff went the Little Red Train.

Click clack went the wheels on the track.

Click clack clicketty clack.

The Little Red Train stopped at Castle Down.
"We're in a hurry," said Duffy Driver, "this train's
for Pebblecombe fair."
A gang of noisy children climbed on board.
Chuff chuff went the Little Red Train.
Chuff chuff, chuffitty chuff...

The next station was Old Harbour.

"Any passengers for Pebblecombe?" called Duffy Driver.

"Is this the right train?" said a boy with a great big dog.

"It is the right train," said Duffy. "And we've no time to lose."

Whoo...eee... whistled the Little Red Train.

Chuff chuff chuffitty chuff.

When they stopped at Hillside station, there were four musicians
waiting on the platform.

"We're playing at Pebblecombe fair," they grumbled,

"and we're going to be late."

"In you get," said Duffy briskly, "we're going as fast as we can."

Whoo...eee... went the Little Red Train. *Whoo...eeee...*

The Little Red Train went faster than ever before.
Click clack went the wheels on the track.
Clicketty clicketty clicketty clack.
"Slow down," said the lady with the strawberries.

"Slow down!" shouted the man with the crate of hens.
"Slow down!" shrieked the boy with the great big dog.
"Steady on!" cried the musicians.
"Faster ... faster!" yelled the noisy children.

But Duffy Driver couldn't hear anyone shouting.
He shovelled more coal into the firebox and
the boiler made more and more steam and
the wheels of the Little Red Train went
faster and faster and faster...
Clicketty clicketty clicketty clicketty clicketty clicketty clack.

And right on time the Little Red Train
pulled into the station at Pebblecombe.

Out got the lady with her box of strawberries, the man with the hens and the boy with the dog and the four musicians and the gang of noisy children.

They thanked Duffy Driver and the
Little Red Train for getting them to
Pebblecombe so fast. Then they all
went off to spend the day at the fair.

Duffy Driver thought he would have another breakfast.
"You're the Little Red Express now," he said as he wiped
down the fenders.
*Whoo…eeee…*went the Little Red Train.
Whoo…oooo…eeee…

More exciting stories to enjoy!

Picture Story Books

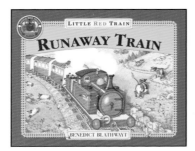

(also available as a Story Book and CD)   (also available as a Story Book and CD)   (also available as a Story Book and CD)

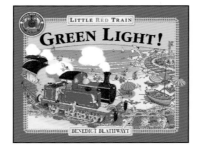
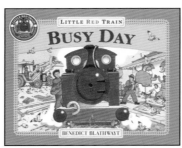

(also available as a Story Book and CD)   (also available as a Story Book and CD)

Gift Books
Stop That Train! – A Pop-Through-the-Slot Book
Little Red Train Adventure Playset
The Runaway Train Pop-up Book
The Runaway Train Sticker Frieze
The Little Red Train Gift Collection
The Runaway Train Book and DVD